MW00889961

Babci's Angel

By Frrich Lewandowski

Illustrations by Kathryn H. Delisle

Ambassador Books
Worcester, Massachusetts

Babci's Angel

Copyright ©1998 by Richard P. Lewandowski

All rights reserved. No part of this book smay be reproduced or transmitted in any form or by any means, electronic or mechanical, including photocopying, recording, or by any information or retrieval system, without written permission from the Publisher.

ISBN: 0-9646439-5-2

Library of Congress Catalog Card Number: 96-96834

Printed in Singapore

Published by: **Ambassador Books, Inc.**
71 Elm Street
Worcester, MA 01609

To order, call: 800 577-0909

*This book is dedicated
to my Babcis
and to Scott Peter,
my family's little angel.*

Frrich

Other books by Frrich Lewandowski:

The First Easter Bunny
Shooting Stardust

Scott and Peter loved their grandparents very much.
While all their friends' grandparents were nice, they all seemed very much the same.

Scott and Peter's grandparents were different. They were special! They were born in a far off country.

They spoke a little differently.

Even their names were different. While all their friends called their grandparents, "Gramma" and "Grandpa," Scott, Peter, and all their cousins called their grandmother "Babci" (Bahb'chee) and their grandfather "Dziadzi" (Jah'jee).

The boys liked their grandparents, and they visited them a lot. In the summer, they would help Dziadzi weed and water his vegetable garden and often water Dziadzi and each other too!

In the fall, they would help Babci make jello or cookies. And when it rained, they enjoyed a special treat. For on rainy days, Babci and Dziadzi would take them up to their attic and show them old toys, old clothes, and old photos.

After the attic tour, they would all enjoy a little snack and then sit in the living room, where Babci and Dziadzi would tell the boys stories about the olden days. Both boys agreed that their favorite story was the one about Babci's angel. And though she told it to them very often, Scott and Peter asked to hear it again and again.

"A long, long time ago when Babci was a little girl," she would begin, "there were no clock radios or alarm clocks." The boys would then ask, "How did you get up on time to go to school or church? Or wake up early on Christmas morning to see what presents Santa left?"

10

Babci would continue. "Every night before she went to bed, Babci knelt down to say her prayers and asked her angel to wake her up on time the next morning. "And every morning at exactly the right time, her angel would come and wiggle her big toe, gently waking her."

11

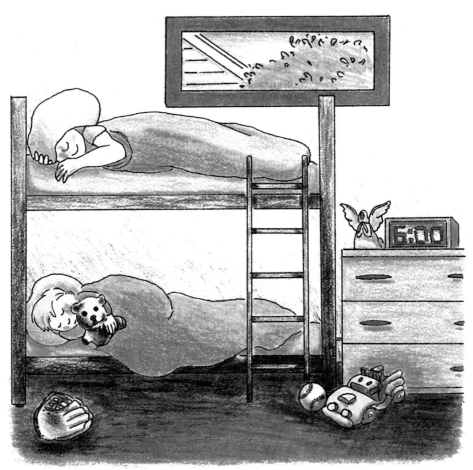

Though times have changed, and Scott and Peter had a clock radio to wake them, Babci always ended the story reminding the two boys that a time might come when they'd need some special help. When that time came, she told them to pray to the angel and the angel would help them too.

It was coming close to Christmas, just two more days to go. Scott and Peter's Mom and Dad needed to go shopping, so they brought the boys to Babci and Dziadzi's for the day. It was snowing quite hard and after the two boys helped Dziadzi shovel the sidewalk, they took the old sled from the garage and took turns sliding down the hill in front of the house.

Sometimes, they'd even slide down together. As they climbed the hill, they'd wave to Babci and Dziadzi who watched from the windows and always smiled. Scott went down the hill alone and steered to the side. "Watch out!" yelled Peter. Scott turned his head to see what Peter wanted and hit a tree, falling from the sled. At first Peter laughed, thinking his brother was fooling around, but his brother didn't move. Dziadzi ran out to him and Babci followed.

An ambulance came and took Scott to the hospital. Babci rode in the ambulance with Scott. After writing a note to the boys' Mom and Dad and leaving it on the table, Dziadzi drove Peter to meet Scott and Babci.

15

Before long, the parents arrived and everyone was crying. The doctors came and spoke to the adults. Peter couldn't really understand what they were talking about but he could tell by the way they looked that they were really scared.

His mother later explained that Scott wasn't waking up and that he was "unconscious." She told him that she and Dad would have to stay the night with Scott at the hospital, but that Peter would sleep at Babci and Dziadzi's and then return in the morning.

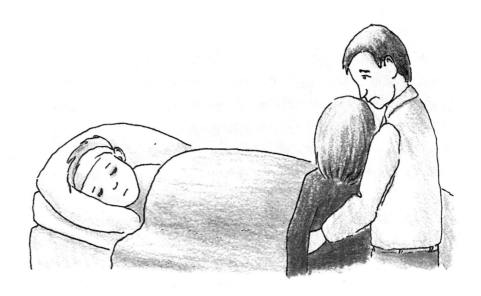

After breakfast, Babci, Dziadzi and Peter returned to find Scott still lying in bed - his mother and father standing by him with tears in their eyes. Peter looked at Scott as he just lay there with black eyes and a bandage on his head.

Then he remembered the story that Babci told. And he began to pray to the angel. "Please wake him up. . . Please wake him up," he prayed over and over.

Just then he looked
at his brother's foot.

The big toe wig-
gled, then
stopped. Again it
wiggled and just
kept wiggling.
"It's Babci's angel,"
Peter shouted. "Look, it's
Babci's angel. Look at his
toe, it's Babci's angel."

They all looked and just then Scott awoke. "Leave my toe alone," he said. His Mom and Dad kept hugging Scott and wouldn't let go. Dziadzi rested his hand on Babci's shoulder. Babci just sat there, closed her eyes and bowed her head. A tear rolled down her cheek. Peter stood next to her, wiped away the tear and whispered in her ear, "I knew your angel would wake Scott up." Babci sat Peter on her lap and hugged him. "I knew it too," she said. "And just in time for Christmas."